THE LEGEND OF PINEAPPLE COVE

POSEIDON'S STORM BLASTER

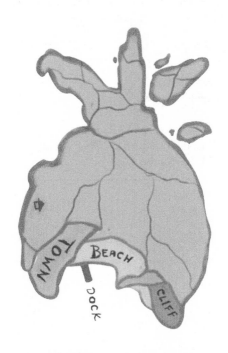

By **Marina J. Bowman**

Illustrated by **Nathan Monção**

JPF
Bowman

First paperback edition May 2019

Written by Marina J. Bowman
Illustrated by Nathan Monção

ISBN 978-1-950341-01-6 (paperback color)
ISBN 978-1-950341-02-3 (paperback black & white)
ISBN 978-1-950341-00-9 (ebook)

Published by Code Pineapple
www.codepineapple.com

For Janet, Frances, and Sharon

ALSO BY MARINA J. BOWMAN

THE LEGEND OF PINEAPPLE COVE

A fantasy-adventure series for kids with bravery, kindness, and friendship. If you like reimagined mythology and animal sidekicks, you'll love this legendary story!

#1 Poseidon's Storm Blaster

#2 A Mermaid's Promise

#3 King of the Sea

#4 Protector's Pledge

SCAREDY BAT

A supernatural detective series for kids with courage, teamwork, and problem solving. If you like solving mysteries and overcoming fears, you'll love this enchanting tale!

#1 Scaredy Bat and the Frozen Vampires

#2 Scaredy Bat and the Sunscreen Snatcher

#3 Scaredy Bat and the Missing Jellyfish

DOWNLOAD THE AUDIOBOOK FREE!

READ THIS FIRST

Just to say thanks for getting my book, I'd like to give

you the Audiobook version 100% FREE!

GET IT HERE:

thelegendofpineapplecove.com/book1

ADVENTURERS

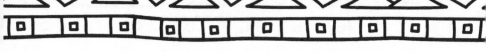

KAI

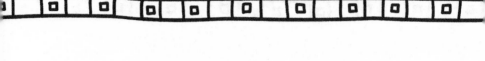

DELPHI

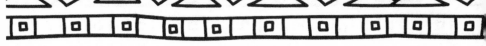

CAPTAIN HOBBS

AUNT CORA

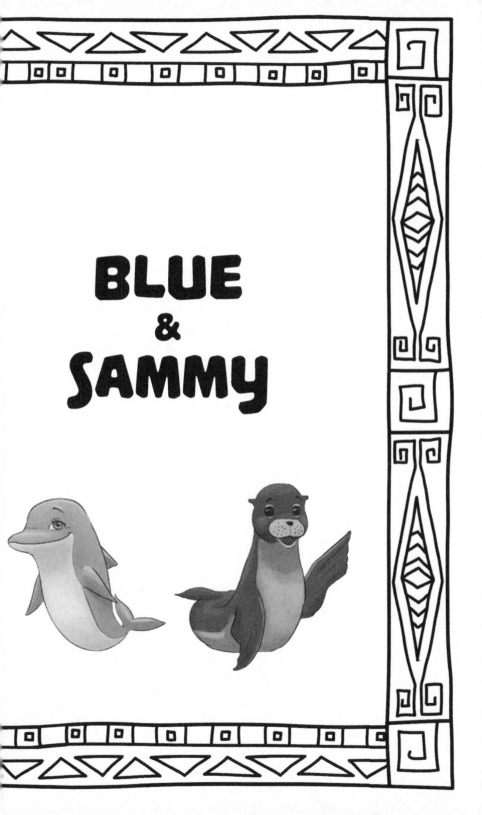

CONTENTS

EXTRAS

HIDDEN PINEAPPLE GAME

While you read, keep an eye out for 14 hidden pineapples in the illustrations. When you're finished, you can check the answer key at the back of the book!

There is a place not far from here
Where big adventures await.
It's a town of magic and monsters and secrets
On an island, in the middle of the salty sea.

Pineapple Cove is its name.
The spot where it all begins.

There, kids can be explorers
And ride ships
And follow tattered, dark maps
And become the heroes
They were always meant to be.

CHAPTER 1

UNLIKELY FRIENDS

Kai was out on the beach that morning, collecting clams. They were salty and delicious, but Kai didn't like collecting them. It was hard work.

First, he would look for dimples in the sand. Then he'd dig and dig and dig until he found the clam. Finally, he'd fill the hole back up with sand. His dad was a fisherman, and that meant Kai went clamming *a lot*.

"Bor-ing," Kai sighed, and plopped another clam in his bright red bucket.

The sand was buttery yellow. The wind was soft and the waves were gentle. It was a beautiful day just like any other. It was Pineapple Cove after all.

"Shoot." Kai had broken another shell. He had a bad habit of hitting the clams with his shovel and cracking them. His dad was always telling him to slow down and be more careful, especially since he had turned ten.

As Kai bent to collect the clam, shouts and laughter rang out across the beach. A group of school kids darted across the beach, joking and kicking up sand.

"Hey!" said Alana, the girl at the front. "There's Kai!" The kids skidded to a halt in front of him, with big grins on their faces.

At least someone's having fun today, Kai thought.

"Hey, Kai," Alana said, flicking back her long, dark hair. "Are you coming to the games tonight? Everyone's going."

He'd forgotten about that! There was an event in the town hall that night, and everyone would be there for the start of summer break. "Sure!" he said, but the kids were already off again, running across the sand.

Kai sighed. He would have given anything to run off with them and leave his bucket of clams behind.

The kids slowed a little up ahead. They stopped. They pointed. They laughed. Kai looked up and squinted, trying to see what they'd found. *Oh, it's Delphi,* he realized.

Delphi was different. She had washed up onshore when she was little. Her only family was her adoptive Aunt Cora. The other townspeople thought Aunt Cora was odd. There were rumors that she had a house full of strange creatures.

The other kids thought Delphi was weird too. She never went in the water. She kept to herself. And she spent all her time with a blubbery sea lion named Sammy.

Right now, Delphi stood on top of a blue bucket with Sammy the sea lion next to her. She spoke to him like he could actually speak back, which was impossible of course.

The other kids laughed and shouted something at her. Delphi's face went red all over, like a big tomato. Finally, they ran off and left her alone.

Delphi fished around in her pocket and brought out some stones, her face shining and angry.

Kai frowned. He picked up his shovel and bucket and walked over to her. "Hey," he called out, "are you OK?"

Delphi didn't answer. Instead, she pulled back her arm and launched a glittering stone into the ocean. "Take that! And that!"

Kai stopped next to her. "Delphi?"

"What?" She said, continuing to throw stones. Sammy made a strange, throaty barking noise next to her. "No, I don't think so, Sammy."

"Um, I saw that the other kids were laughing and pointing at you."

"And you want to laugh and point too?" Delphi asked, tossing another stone. Sammy sniffed Kai's bucket of clams and licked his lips.

"No! I just wanted to check that you were OK."

Before Delphi could answer, a soft cry came from the ocean.

"What was that?" Kai and Delphi asked at the same time. Sammy whimpered and flopped backward on his flippers, hiding behind Delphi.

CHAPTER 2

GIFT FROM THE SEA

The sound came from the direction of a stone archway jutting out of the water. Kai sometimes fished near it with his father.

Delphi squinted at the sea and pointed. "There! It's a baby dolphin! It sounds like it's in trouble!"

Kai dropped his bucket of clams. "We've got to help it. Come on!"

But Delphi didn't move. "I c-can't. I can't go in the water."

"Then I'll go." Kai waded through the water. He crashed into the waves, and the waves crashed into him. Kai was a great swimmer.

Kai reached the dolphin in no time. It had

sleek, bluish-gray skin. A net was hooked over its long nose. Kai gently placed his hand on the dolphin. "Hey, it's OK, Blue. Can I call you that? You'll be OK."

Kai bobbed in the salt water and untied the net. The dolphin squeaked in relief and dove into the water. It was free!

As Kai swam back to shore, the dolphin popped up next to him. This time it had something shiny in its mouth.

"What do you have, Blue?" Kai opened his hand, and Blue dropped the item in his palm.

Kai gasped. It was a gold trident necklace!

Blue chirp-clicked, did a happy little flip, and disappeared beneath the waves. Kai swam back to the beach and rejoined Delphi.

"That was brave of you, Kai." Delphi wiggled her toes atop the bucket. "I'm sorry I didn't help. I'm...afraid of the water. I have been for a long time."

"It's OK. Why are you afraid of the water?" Kai asked.

Delphi twisted her fingers through the rope around her waist. "I'm sure you already know, but…I washed up on shore when I was little. I don't remember much, but every time I go near water I get a bit…itchy. And scared. I can't swim…or I could and I don't remember." Delphi shook her head. "It doesn't matter. What's that in your hand?"

"Oh, yeah!" Kai showed Delphi the trident necklace and told her what had happened.

"It's a gift from the sea. You should put it on!" Delphi smiled, opening her arms wide. Sammy barked in agreement.

Kai's fingers tingled as he lifted the necklace. A gust of wind ruffled his hair, and the sun, which had disappeared behind some clouds, reappeared. A circle of light fell around Kai. He slipped the trident necklace over his head. It was heavier than he expected, and warm against his wet skin.

"Wow," Delphi said, standing on tiptoe on her bucket. "I wonder how the dolphin found it. Or where it came from."

"I don't know, but it's pretty cool."

"You can say that again."

"It's pretty–"

BONG-BONG-BONG! A bell clanged three times, loud and clear, from the town square.

"What's going on? Three bells are for emergencies, right?" Delphi asked.

"We'd better go find out," Kai said.

Together they ran back to their town, with Sammy flippering along close behind.

CHAPTER 3

THE MESSAGE

Kai and Delphi hurried into Pineapple Cove. They ran past the baker's shop, where smells of yummy fresh bread drifted out. They ran past the coffee shop and the florist's, but everything was quiet.

Finally, they rushed into the town square. There was a crowd of a hundred people gathered in front of the town hall. On the stage, right at the front of it, stood the mayor.

He held a piece of crinkly parchment in his hand. Carl, the messenger pelican, was perched awkwardly on his shoulder. The mayor cleared his throat, and Carl ruffled his pinky-white feathers. "Carl has just delivered this message from one of the ships out at sea."

Kai moved closer to the stage. His dad's fishing ship was out at sea.

"Dear Mayor," the mayor read, while Carl pecked at the mayor's hair. "Something terrible has happened, and we are writing this letter to warn the people of Pineapple Cove."

Whispers rushed through the crowd.

The mayor continued reading. "It was a normal morning. All our poles were out over

13

the side of the boat. We had just caught a gigantic fish, and then…it happened."

"What happened?" someone called out.

"The ship started rocking from one side to the other." The mayor's eyes were round as coconuts now. "And then there was a big *CRASH*."

Carl ruffled his feathers, slip-sliding on the mayor's fancy jacket.

The mayor read further. "A giant octopus monster attacked our ship! Its tentacles crushed

our mast, and it ate our fish."

"Oh no!" someone yelled. A man in the crowd fainted.

The mayor continued. "We were able to escape from the ship on one of the lifeboats."

A sigh of relief swept through the crowd. Kai relaxed a little – his dad was safe. But a giant octopus monster?

The mayor raised his hand and quieted everyone. "But now the monster is headed directly for Pineapple Cove!" The mayor stopped reading. He looked around at the crowd.

"This is terrible!" someone yelled.

"What are we going to do?" someone else asked.

"Everyone calm down," the mayor said, as he tried to push Carl off his shoulder. But the panicked shouting continued.

Kai and Delphi hurried through the crowd, their stomachs squiggled up with fear. Sammy the sea lion flopped along behind them, barking all the way.

CHAPTER 4

TIME TO PREPARE

Kai was determined to find his mom and younger sister. Delphi needed to find her aunt. They ran through the crowd, past the panicking adults.

"Why is this happening?" the baker shouted.

"What can we do against a sea monster?" the florist asked.

"My house is right on the water!" the coffee shop owner yelled.

"*All* our houses are on the water!" the baker responded.

"We need to come up with a plan," a woman said, calmly. That was Kai's mom! He ran over to her and gave her a big hug. She had Kai's

younger sister, Maya, with her. Delphi's Aunt
Cora stood beside them, clutching her seaweed
purse.

On the stage, the mayor cleared his throat.
He held out his hands. "Everyone calm down,
please."

Next to Kai, Aunt Cora shifted and cast a
glance in his direction. Her eyes twinkled, and
her gaze fixed on his trident necklace. There

was a gasp as Aunt Cora ran and jumped on stage next to the mayor.

"We need Captain Hobbs!" Aunt Cora shouted, waving her arms. "He's the Protector for Pineapple Cove. He can help us with the sea monster."

A few of the kids nearby rolled their eyes. Alana, who had been on the beach that morning, sniggered at Delphi.

"Hobbs won't help us. He turned his back on us long ago," a man muttered.

"Yeah, I haven't seen him around in ages," a woman said.

The mayor guided Aunt Cora off the stage. "Everyone must go home and prepare for the attack as best as possible," he said. "That's all we can do right now."

"When will it come?" Kai's mom asked.

"The fishing ship was less than a day away when it was attacked," the mayor replied, glancing at the crinkly paper again. "We must be ready, right away."

More shouts broke out, but Kai had stopped listening. A wave of heat rushed through him.

He wanted to find the sea monster himself. To protect his village. To get even with the sea monster for attacking his dad's boat. He looked over at his mom and sister and calmed down a little. No, he should stay and help protect the house. What could he do against a sea monster, anyway?

The kids from school rushed past, but a few of them slowed. "Delphi, you're so weird. And your aunt is too. Do you really think some lame captain will help us?" Alana said.

"Don't talk about my aunt like that," Delphi said, folding her arms. "You might not believe her, but I do."

"What do you think, Kai?" Alana asked.

Kai froze. Sammy the sea lion gave an encouraging bark. "I–um–" He didn't want to lie, but he didn't want to hurt Delphi's feelings either.

"Oh, whatever. Come on, guys," Alana said and ran off with the others, still laughing at what Aunt Cora had said.

"You don't believe my aunt?" Delphi asked Kai, a big frown wrinkling up her olive forehead.

"It's not that I don't believe her. It's just that I need to make sure my house is protected in case the monster attacks. You heard the mayor. It could come at any moment."

"Fine," Delphi said. A heavy silence hung between them.

Finally, Kai's mom and Aunt Cora rejoined them and broke the silence.

"Kai, it's time to go home and prepare the house." Kai's mom looked from Kai to Delphi and back again. "And once we're finished, why don't you go help Delphi with her house? What do you think, Cora?"

Aunt Cora smiled mischievously. "That would be lovely."

Kai eyed Delphi, but she was staring at the ground. "OK, sure."

"Wonderful," Kai's mom said. "Let's get to it."

Kai followed his mom and Maya to their house, and Delphi followed Aunt Cora to their house. It was time to prepare for the sea monster attack.

CHAPTER 5

AUNT CORA'S HOUSE

Kai made quick work of preparing his family's house. They closed up shutters, and he helped his mom place wood planks over the doors. They packed away anything that could get broken or tossed around in the house.

As soon as they were done, Kai set off to Aunt Cora's house to do the same for her. Aunt Cora's house was weathered – a brick home with a front porch and a seashell stepping stone path.

The speckled front door opened, and Aunt Cora stepped out. She held a large iguana the length of her arm. "Hello, Kai," she said.

* * *

"Come inside and have something to eat. You must be hungry after all that work at your house." There was still that strange twinkle in her eye.

Kai followed Aunt Cora inside, his heart beating a little faster than usual. He stopped inside the doorway. He could barely believe his eyes.

The inside of Aunt Cora's house was filled with nests and habitats, each one with a different creature inside. There were ancient turtles and glowing frogs. There was a tank with a beautiful blue fish inside. There was a bubbling tube in the center of the room, filled with seaweed and starfish. There were birds with sharp beaks and necks that were too long. There was a curious monkey sitting on top of a perch in the corner.

Sammy the sea lion barked and flip-flopped over to a big circular pool next to a set of wooden stairs. He dived into it and splashed water everywhere.

"Whoa," Kai said, shaking his head. He had never seen so many creatures in one place before.

Aunt Cora laughed and came closer. She tapped on the bubbling tube. A strange fish, with eyes that were far too bright and smart, swooshed into view and flapped a fin at them. It smiled, or so it seemed, and revealed a mouth full of wickedly sharp teeth.

"This is Finley," she said. "Say 'hello,' Finley." Finley the fish waved his tail at them.

"He-hello," Kai stammered.

"Don't be scared, Kai. All the creatures here are safe," Aunt Cora said. Kai relaxed and moved closer to Finley's tank.

"Well, as long as they're not hungry," Aunt

Cora added. "And come to think of it, Finley's always hungry, so make sure not to stick your fingers in his tank." Finley smiled. Kai gulped.

Aunt Cora motioned to Kai. He followed her and entered a small dining room with shining seashell counters, a table, and four mismatched chairs. Delphi was at the table, paging through a book called *Creatures of the Deep.*

Kai sat down across from Delphi while Aunt Cora prepared them lunch in the kitchen.

"Hey," Kai said. Delphi looked up, then went back to flipping through the book.

Kai tried again, lowering his voice. "I'm sorry about earlier…with Alana and the other kids. I don't think your aunt is crazy. I just don't know about this Captain Hobbs."

Delphi looked up again and stared at Kai. Finally, she nodded and said, "Thanks."

"For what?" Kai asked.

"None of the other kids have ever apologized to me. Or been nice to me." Delphi smiled. Kai smiled back.

The smell of grilled fish and chips drifted

through the room. Kai's stomach growled.

"I'm starving," Kai said.

"Meeee too," Delphi agreed.

"Me three!" Aunt Cora said as she walked over. She set down plates of delicious fish and chips in front of them. Kai and Delphi thanked Aunt Cora and dug into their food.

"Guess what happened to us today, Aunt Cora?" Delphi said with a mouthful of chips.

"What is it, my starfish?"

"Kai saved a dolphin from a fishing net today!"

"Ah! So that's where you got the trident necklace from," Aunt Cora said.

"Wait. How did you know that?" Kai asked.

Aunt Cora didn't answer. She bustled out of the room, her footsteps clunking on the stone floor. She was back in no time, carrying a leatherbound book. She plopped it down in the middle of the table and opened it up.

She pointed to a sketch of a man with a grizzly beard and a captain's hat. Around his neck hung a…

"Trident necklace!" Kai exclaimed.

"This is Captain Hobbs," Aunt Cora said. "He was a Protector of Pineapple Cove for the longest time. Actually, he was one of Poseidon's Protectors of the Seventh Sea. Pineapple Cove was the home base for all of the Protectors."

Aunt Cora smiled. "I still remember when he first came back to town, carrying a sack full of crystals from one of his adventures. Whenever there was trouble in town, he was there to help." The smile on her face faded. "Until one day…"

"What happened?" Kai asked.

"I'm not sure exactly. All I know is that he disappeared when the town needed him most. Then he turned up at the Broken Barrel Pub several months later and has been there ever since."

"Do you think the necklace is connected to these Protectors?" Delphi asked.

"It might be," Aunt Cora said mysteriously.

So many questions filled Kai's head at once. *What does a Protector do? And how do*

you become one? What happened to Captain Hobbs? The captain seemed to be the key. He might even help them defeat the sea monster.

"Where is the Broken Barrel Pub?" Kai asked. "Just curious."

Aunt Cora raised an eyebrow. "It's right off the trade route, two nautical miles southeast of here. Not far at all."

That settles it, Kai thought. He would go find the captain and bring him to Pineapple Cove. His stomach went floopsy with excitement.

Delphi eyed Kai suspiciously. Kai cleared his throat. "So how can I help with preparing the house?"

Aunt Cora smiled. "We've done just about everything we can do to prepare. But thank you for your kind offer, dear."

Kai wolfed down the rest of his lunch. "I should head home. My mom will be expecting me soon." Kai thanked Aunt Cora and said goodbye to her and Delphi. But Kai didn't head home. Instead he hurried toward the dock, where his dad kept their small sailboat.

CHAPTER 6

A RECKLESS MISTAKE

J ust as Kai was about to push the boat into the water, a bark sounded behind him.

"Wait!" Delphi jogged up to him and Sammy flopped next to her. "You can't go find Captain Hobbs by yourself. You need to make a plan first."

"Sure I can," Kai said. "I know where he is and how to get there."

"But...did you plan a route? Do you know what you're going to say if you find him?" Delphi asked.

"I'll figure it out," Kai said as the bow of the boat slid into the water. "And if you're so worried, you should come along with me."

Delphi looked at the waves bumping up against the boat. "Um…are you a good sailor? I-is it safe?"

Kai put his hands on his hips. "I'm the best. It's perfectly safe."

"OK. I guess it's fine as long as I don't have to touch the water." Delphi turned and ran up the beach.

"Huh? Where is she going?" Kai scratched his head. Sammy barked, sharing his confusion.

Delphi reappeared, and Kai coughed to keep from laughing. "What are you wearing?"

Delphi had put about twenty floaty devices on her arms and legs. She handed one to Kai. "Just in case," she said.

Delphi moved toward the boat carefully, and Kai helped her inside. Sammy splashed in after her. Delphi settled in and tucked her bag against her side. "Let's go!" she cried.

Kai pushed the boat all the way into the water and hopped inside. The sail puffed out, and they moved steadily away from shore.

"So how are we going to get to the Broken

Barrel Pub?" Delphi asked. The boat continued to float away from the beach.

"Easy, I just have to use the stars. My dad taught me how…oh, wait. There are no stars out yet." Kai's shoulders slumped. They drifted further away from land. He looked at Delphi, expecting her to freak out.

"I'm sorry, I guess I should have thought things through more. I'll turn us around," Kai said. He started to adjust the sails.

"Well, can we use this?" Delphi pulled out a round object from her bag.

Kai looked in Delphi's hands. "A compass! Yes! We can use that." Kai exhaled. Delphi handed him the compass.

Kai studied the compass. "Thanks! You were right, planning was a good idea." He turned the boat to face southeast.

Delphi's cheeks turned pink. "You're welcome. Do you want to talk about what we should say when we find Captain Hobbs?"

"Yeah, let's do it," Kai said.

While the two bounced around ideas, Kai made sure they sailed in the right direction. Delphi made sure the water stayed put. And Sammy made sure they had fishy snacks for their journey.

CHAPTER 7

THE MYSTERIOUS RED X

Kai and Delphi approached the tiniest island they'd ever seen. In fact, it was more of a large rock sticking out of the water. On top of the rock sat an enormous teetering ship.

At last, they rocked up against a barrel jetty, and Kai helped Delphi out of the boat. A long line of barrels strung together led right up to the ship.

"The Broken Barrel looks just like a broken old ship," Kai said, "but with a door." A rumbling noise nearby made Kai jump. "What's that?"

Delphi giggled and put a finger to her lips.

She pointed to Sammy, who was curled up in the bottom of their boat, snoring peacefully.

"You know, this ship used to carry Piña Pop along the Ananas trade route. But then it crashed into this tiny island, and it's been stuck here ever since," Delphi whispered as they tied their little boat to a barrel.

"Yeah, my dad told me the Broken Barrel is a popular place for fishermen to stop for food and drinks," Kai said.

They set off across the barrels, hopping from one to the other, their flip-flops squidging against the sun-baked wood.

As they got closer, the noises of people singing and laughing reached their ears. They hopped off the last barrel and entered the pub with a creak of its moldy wooden door.

The sights, sounds, and smells of the Broken Barrel hit them right away. The pub was filled with sailors and seafarers of all kinds. Kai and Delphi scanned the room, looking for Captain Hobbs.

A large man had his head on the table and looked like he was taking an afternoon nap. A small man performed a card trick. A group of men and women had their arms linked together and sang a merry song. The smell of Piña Pop filled Kai and Delphi's noses. A lady with an eye patch cleaned glasses behind the bar. Kai guessed that she was the captain of the Broken Barrel.

At last they spotted someone familiar, sitting in the corner with his head down. The man barely looked like the one from Aunt Cora's drawing. He had wrinkles under his eyes and much of his face was hidden behind a grizzly gray beard and a hat.

Kai and Delphi approached him. "Captain Hobbs? Is that you?" Kai asked.

"Who's asking?" Captain Hobbs grumbled.

"I'm Kai, and this is Delphi. Pineapple Cove is in danger. We need your help."

"I can't help you," Captain Hobbs grumbled again. He didn't even look up at them.

"Come on, Captain," Delphi said, folding her arms. "We know you're the Protector for Pineapple Cove. A sea monster is coming. You have to help."

The captain sighed. "I used to be. But then I made an unforgivable mistake."

"What mistake? What happened?" Kai asked.

"Terrible, terrible mistake," the captain repeated.

Kai wouldn't give up. "If you can't help us yourself, please tell us how to defeat the monster."

"It's impossible. The answer you seek is locked away. And to find the key, you must perform a selfless act of bravery. Only then will the trident key appear."

Kai and Delphi looked at each other. "You mean like this?" Kai held out the sparkling trident necklace.

Finally, the captain raised his head. His eyes were blue and bright. He stared at the necklace in stunned silence. "How…where did you get that?"

Hope returned to the captain's face. He touched his finger to the trident and said, "I think I may be able to help you after all."

"You can?" Delphi grinned. "I knew it!"

"Kai saved a dolphin from a fishing net. Then the dolphin gave him the necklace!" Delphi put her hands on her hips.

Hobbs glanced around the crowded bar and leaned forward. Kai and Delphi moved closer to his table. "Pineapple Cove has a secret."

"What's the secret?" asked Kai.

"Pineapple Cove is home to a magic portal that leads to Poseidon's temple. Inside the temple is an ancient artifact infused with the power of the king of the sea himself. The artifact is called Poseidon's Storm Blaster."

Hobbs reached into his pocket and pulled out a wrinkled old map. "Here." He pressed his finger to a big red X. "This is where the portal is located."

Kai stared at the X. "Hey, this is near where my dad takes me fishing."

Hobbs nodded. "This is where you need to go. Once you have the Storm Blaster, you can defeat the sea monster."

Kai looked at Delphi and remembered his mistake with the compass. He wasn't sure he was the right person for this mission.

"Captain, maybe *you* should have the trident necklace. You can use it to get the Storm Blaster and protect Pineapple Cove." Kai lifted the necklace off his neck and offered it to Hobbs.

Captain Hobbs shook his head. "No, the necklace is yours. It was sent to you because of your selfless act. It means you've been invited to become a Junior Protector. I believe you are meant for this task."

"And so do I!" Delphi exclaimed.

"OK." Kai nodded to Delphi. This might be their only chance to save Pineapple Cove.

They had to do it. "Let's go!" Kai pointed to the door and lifted the map.

Kai and Delphi started to walk off, but Captain Hobbs' chair scraped the floor. "Wait," he said. "I will come with you. This mission may not be mine, but I can still help. Pineapple Cove was once my home too."

Together, Hobbs, Kai, Delphi, and Sammy boarded the captain's ship. They set sail toward Pineapple Cove, in search of the mysterious red X.

CHAPTER 8

THE GUARDIANS OF POSEIDON'S TEMPLE

In no time at all, they reached the location of the magic portal.

"We have arrived," said Hobbs triumphantly.

"It's here?" Kai asked, as they sailed toward the stone archway, just off Pineapple Cove's coast. Delphi sat on the side of the boat now, and actually dipped a finger into the water.

"It's not so bad," she muttered. A bit of it splashed on her arm and she let out a little cry. She laughed.

Captain Hobbs nodded. "Yes, this is the portal."

Kai didn't understand. This was the same old rock archway that everyone knew about. In fact, Kai had sailed underneath it before with his father.

How could it be a magical opening to Poseidon's Island?

"Come, Kai," Hobbs said, nudging him forward. "Go to the front of the boat, hold your trident necklace, and say, 'By Poseidon's invitation, let me pass.'"

The captain didn't seem like one to make jokes, so Kai did as he was told. He hurried to the front of the boat, squishing past Delphi. They sailed toward the rock archway. Sammy covered his eyes with a moist flipper.

"By Poseidon's invitation," Kai said, holding out his necklace. "Let me pass."

There was a shimmery flash. The space under the archway turned purplish-blue and transparent. The boat sailed through it and out the other side.

An island that surely hadn't been there a moment before appeared in front of them.

Captain Hobbs sailed up to it and stopped the boat. He let down a wooden plank onto the sand. "This is Poseidon's Island," Captain Hobbs said. "I must wait with the ship. You two get the Storm Blaster."

Kai and Delphi slid down the plank together. Sammy followed them. Delphi didn't cry even once, though she still had her floatation devices on. She even waded through the shallow water on the beach to get to the sand.

"Look over there." Delphi pointed to a temple ahead of them.

Squiggly pictures were scratched on the outside. The dark entrance glowed a soft blue.

"Here we go," Kai said. Delphi followed him, stripping off the floaties as she walked. They stopped in front of the entrance.

The temple was dark, and they couldn't see what was inside. Strange echoes floated out to them. Kai and Delphi each took a deep breath and stepped forward.

The inside of the temple was lit by blue orbs that hung from the ceiling by strips of seaweed. Statues of people with tridents lined the walls.

They walked on and found a massive doorway inside the temple. On either side of the glittering bronze doors stood two blue people. Royal blue from head to toe. They had pointy ears and webbed fingers. They wore stern expressions and held spears in their hands.

"We are the guardians of Poseidon's temple. What is your purpose here?" one of the guards asked, pointing the spear at Kai.

Kai cleared his throat. "I am Kai of Pineapple Cove. We're here for the Storm Blaster," he said. "Our town is in danger from a horrible octopus monster."

The two guards looked at each other. The blue woman on the left wrinkled up her nose. "I see you possess the trident necklace. That means you are pure of heart."

The other guard nodded. "You may enter."

"That's it? You'll let us pass, just like that?" Delphi asked. Sammy barked and flippered up to her side.

"Only Kai may enter, as he possesses the trident necklace," the guards said.

Delphi frowned and looked down at the floor.

Kai stepped forward. "She's with me. I wouldn't be here if it weren't for her. Please let Delphi and Sammy come too."

The guards stared at them for a while and then finally stepped back. The blue woman opened the doors to the room.

It was dark in there. Scary, even. Kai wasn't afraid of much, but the temple was seriously creepy.

Could they really do this? Delphi nodded toward the room.

Kai nodded back at Delphi, and they walked through the doorway together.

The doors slammed shut behind them. They were plunged into darkness. Sammy gave a little whine at their side.

CHAPTER 9

FROM THE OCEANS COLD
AND WARM

Up ahead, on a pedestal in a circle of light, sat a crystal case. Inside the crystal case was the Storm Blaster.

"There it is," Kai whispered, holding his trident necklace.

"How do we get to it?" asked Delphi. Water surrounded the pedestal, and there were no steps across.

Kai started forward, ready to jump into the water and swim across, but then he stopped. He looked back at Delphi, remembering what happened when he didn't think things through before.

Kai crouched at the edge of the water. He dipped his finger into the pool and swirled it around. The water bubbled and churned. Kai jumped back. Dozens of bright eyes and sharp teeth appeared in the water.

"It's a whole family of Finleys!" gasped Delphi. "But bigger!"

"What do we do?" Kai asked, backing away from the water.

Sammy barked next to Kai, and he looked around, frowning.

The sea lion chewed on the rope around Delphi's waist. "Sammy, this is serious, and all you can think about is snack time?"

Sammy barked twice and nudged the rope again. "Oh! The rope! We can use it to get the Storm Blaster!" Delphi said.

Delphi quickly untied the rope from her waist. She made a lasso out of it and tossed it toward the ceiling. It fell back down with a thud. She tossed it up again, and it fell to the floor again. She threw it harder and pulled, roping one of the hanging blue orbs.

"Ah ha!" Delphi yelled. She offered the rope to Kai. "Here, you can swing across to the pedestal using this rope. Unlock the glass case with the trident key. Then swing back across on the rope. Easy-peasy."

Kai looked at the rope. "Are you sure that will work?"

Delphi gave a little tug on the rope. "Almost positive."

"OK, I'll do it." Kai took the rope from Delphi and faced the water. He ran and jumped, swinging toward the pedestal. The Finleys jumped out of the water and snapped at Kai's ankles, just missing him. He landed on the pedestal. Delphi and Sammy cheered.

Kai stepped up to the crystal case. A lock sat on top of it with three prongs. Kai placed his trident necklace in it. There was a click-hiss, and the case's lid slid open.

The Storm Blaster glistened inside, hovering in mid-air. Carefully, Kai removed it. He tucked the Blaster under one arm and grabbed the rope with both hands. He swung back across. Kai had almost made it to the other side when he felt the Storm Blaster slipping. It slipped down and down until...*splash*! It fell into the water below.

"Oh no!" Kai yelled.

Delphi ran to the water's edge and bent down. "Bad Finley!" she said, as she swatted one of the fish away. She grabbed the Storm Blaster before it sank to the bottom.

Kai landed next to Delphi and pulled her back from the hungry fish. His heart thumped inside his chest.

Delphi finally caught her breath. "See, easy-peasy." She and Kai laughed. Delphi handed the blaster back to Kai.

The doors to the room swung open, and the two blue guardians stepped through. They slammed their spears down once. "Well done," said the blue man, pointing to the glass case. "You have outsmarted our man-eating fish and retrieved the Storm Blaster."

He pointed to the blaster in Kai's hands. "The Storm Blaster holds the power of the sea. With it you can calm any water-loving creature.

It can be shared with others who are worthy."

The blue woman nodded and said, "To activate the Storm Blaster, you must say…"

'From the oceans cold and warm,

I summon Poseidon's storm.'

"Do you understand?"

"I think so. Thank you," Kai said to the blue guardians.

"C'mon, Kai!" Delphi tugged on his arm. "We have to get back to the boat and through the portal before it's too late!"

CHAPTER 10

THE MONSTER

Delphi, Kai, Sammy, and Captain Hobbs sailed back through the portal, quick as they could. The sun was just dipping down in the sky. The water was calm. Pineapple Cove's beaches were peaceful.

"We're here!" Delphi held onto the railing. "And everything is fine. I don't see any monsters."

Kai grinned at her. "You seem more comfortable near the water now."

"Yeah, I'm starting to get used to it. I have to, or else I'll miss out on everything," Delphi said.

Suddenly the boat rocked to the right. It rocked to the left. The wood groaned, and then...*BOOM*!

Kai rushed to the railing. He leaned over and looked down into the deep blue sea.

"Oh no!" Kai yelled.

A giant octopus monster bashed the side of the boat with its tentacles. *Boom-boom-bash.*

Kai wobbled. He hugged the Storm Blaster to his chest. He tipped forward and...*SPLASH*!

"Kai!" Delphi gasped. Kai banged his head on the side of the ship and started to sink.

Captain Hobbs stood at the wheel. He twisted it this way and that. "Delphi! I have to steer us away from the monster."

"But Kai fell in!" Delphi shouted. And I can't go in the water, she thought.

But she had to do something. She untied the rope from around her waist again and made a lasso. She tried to loop it around Kai, but he was completely under the water now.

Delphi looked down at her sea lion friend. "Sammy, quick! Dive in and save Kai!"

But Sammy shook his head. He was afraid of the octopus monster. There was nothing else to do. Delphi was still afraid of the water, but she couldn't let anything happen to Kai.

Delphi took a deep breath and climbed over the railing.

She counted, "One, two, three!"

She dove into the water. It was icy cold.

Delphi kicked her legs. She splashed her arms. She opened her eyes and she swam. *I'm doing it! I'm swimming!*

Delphi found Kai sinking down toward the bottom of the ocean. His eyes were closed.

She grabbed him. There was another splash, and Sammy appeared. He grabbed Delphi's arm in his mouth and pulled on it. He dragged Delphi and Kai to the surface.

Delphi patted Kai on the cheeks. "Wake up!"

Kai choked and spluttered. "Delphi, you're in the water!"

"I know!" There wasn't much time to talk. The sea monster had spotted them. It gave a horrible roar and detached from the boat. It squelched toward them.

Kai and Delphi grabbed onto Sammy, and he swam them to the beach. "Thanks Sammy," Kai said, turning toward the octopus monster.

The monster was closer to shore now, ready to chomp them up. Its beaky mouth appeared, its tentacles flopping onto the beach. One landed right next to Kai's foot.

"Oh no you don't." Kai raised the Storm Blaster. "From the oceans cold and warm, I summon Poseidon's storm." The blaster glowed white and shook in Kai's hands.

Kai pumped the handle with all his might. A swirling stream shot out of the end of the blaster. And it hit the monster right in the face.

The sea monster stopped. It turned and blinked. It shook its tentacles. In fact, it looked as if it had just woken up from a Sunday afternoon nap.

Finally, it slothered off to sea.

"That cooled it off," Delphi joked.

Sammy gave a terrific bark. Kai grinned. Delphi laughed, pushing wet hair back from her forehead.

Cheers rang out from the town. The people of Pineapple Cove ran down the beach. Kai's mom and dad hugged him tightly. Aunt Cora wrapped her arms around Delphi.

Captain Hobbs came down from the boat. "It looks like Pineapple Cove has a new Junior Protector." He winked at Kai.

Aunt Cora put her hand on Hobbs' shoulder. "Welcome back, Captain." Hobbs tipped his hat at Cora.

The mayor walked up to Aunt Cora. "It seems you may have been right, Cora. Next time we'll have to listen to you more carefully." Carl the pelican bobbed his head in agreement.

"I appreciate that, Mr. Mayor," Aunt Cora said.

The fishermen from the lifeboat raised Kai and Delphi in the air.

"I wonder why the sea monster attacked. It looked like it was under a spell," Delphi said.

It didn't matter now. The monster was gone. And Kai would have the Storm Blaster if it came back.

Thanks to Kai's bold stand-off and Delphi's brave swim, Pineapple Cove was safe.

CHAPTER 11

JUNIOR PROTECTORS OF PINEAPPLE COVE

The following morning, everything was peaceful in Pineapple Cove. The waves washed against the butter-yellow shore. Delphi and Kai walked along the beach. Delphi held the bucket, and Kai worked the shovel. Together, they dug for clams and laughed at Sammy.

The sea lion splashed in and out of the water, barking every now and again.

"See, if we dig a hole *next to* where the clam is, we don't break as many shells."

Kai grinned. "Thanks for helping me. I'm going to need all the help I can get soon. Captain Hobbs is going to train me as a Junior Protector!"

"Wow. That's so cool," Delphi replied. "Well, I'll help you with clamming any time you want."

Kai was lucky to have Delphi as a friend, and he gave her another smile to show it. Sammy flippered around nearby, barking happily.

In the distance, a group of kids ran up to them, headed by Alana. Delphi stopped clamming and bit her bottom lip.

"Hi guys," Alana said, waving at them. "Are you coming to the games tonight? The mayor said we can do them now that the sea monster is gone."

Delphi and Kai exchanged a glance. "Sure," they said together.

Alana and the others rushed off again, chatting amongst themselves. For once, they didn't point or laugh at Delphi and Sammy.

"OK, so we can go to–" Kai started.

"What's that?" Delphi asked.

A clickety-chirp had interrupted them. They both looked out at the ocean.

"It's Blue!" Kai shouted. Blue the dolphin flipped out of the water and swam closer to shore. Kai and Delphi rushed out to meet her.

"What have you got there, Blue?" Delphi asked. The dolphin opened its mouth. Inside it was a purple trident necklace. Delphi gasped and took it from the dolphin. "For me?" she asked.

"You deserve it," Kai replied. "You saved the Storm Blaster from the Finleys. And you jumped into the water to save me." Delphi slipped the necklace over her head. A gust of wind blew her hair and the sun shone brighter.

Together, they jogged back to shore and waved at Blue. The dolphin dove back into the ocean. Sammy chased after her, but gave up after a while and came back.

"Now I can train with Captain Hobbs too!" Delphi said, holding her necklace. "I wonder what else we don't know about this island."

"Yeah, I get the feeling that we're just beginning to discover its secrets." Kai and Delphi linked arms and walked back to the clam bucket together. They were Junior Protectors of Pineapple Cove.

HIDDEN PINEAPPLE ANSWER KEY

There are 14 pineapples hidden throughout the illustrations in this story. Did you spot them all?

CHAPTER 1 =
CHAPTER 2 =
CHAPTER 3 =
CHAPTER 4 =
CHAPTER 5 =
CHAPTER 6 =
CHAPTER 7 =
CHAPTER 8 =
CHAPTER 9 = NONE
CHAPTER 10 =
CHAPTER 11 = NONE

Hi!

Did you enjoy the story?

I know I did!

If you want to join the team as we go on more adventures, then leave a review!

Otherwise, we won't know if you're up for the next mission. And when we set out on the journey,

you may never get to hear about it!

You can leave a review wherever you found the book.

The gang and I are excited to see you on the next adventure!

Hopefully there are snacks . . .

The fantastical adventures of Kai and Delphi in
The Legend of Pineapple Cove

Also by Marina J. Bowman:
Scaredy Bat

To learn more, visit thelegendofpineapplecove.com/book1

Don't miss
The Legend of Pineapple Cove #2
A Mermaid's Promise

With a mysterious note as their only clue, Kai and Delphi must journey to the underwater world of the mermaids and rescue Kai's family, before time runs out.

Order now!

thelegendofpineapplecove.com/book1

QUESTIONS FOR DISCUSSION

1. What did you enjoy about this book?

2. What are some of the major themes of this story?

3. How are Kai and Delphi similar? How are they different? How did they help each other in the story?

4. What doubts or fears did the characters express in the book? When have you been afraid? How have you dealt with your fears?

5. The Legend of Pineapple Cove Book #1 ends with some loose ends. What do you think will happen in the next book in the series?

For more Discussion Questions, visit

thelegendofpineapplecove.com/book1

Question 1:

What did you enjoy about this book?

_____

_____

_____

_____

_____

_____

_____

_____

Question 2:

What are some of the major themes of this story?

_____

_____

_____

_____

_____

_____

_____

Question 3:

How are Kai and Delphi similar? How are they different? How did they help each other in the story?

_____

_____

_____

_____

_____

_____

_____

Question 4:

What doubts or fears did the characters express in the book? When have you been afraid? How have you dealt with your fears?

_____

_____

_____

_____

_____

_____

_____

Question 5:

The Legend of Pineapple Cove Book #1 ends with some loose ends. What do you think will happen in the next book in the series?

_____

_____

_____

_____

_____

_____

_____

COLOR IN YOUR OWN JOURNEY!

DESIGN YOUR OWN TRIDENT NECKLACE!

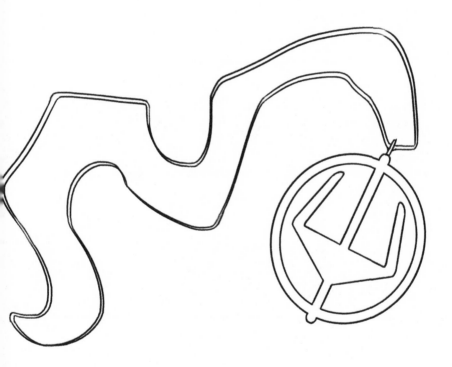

ADD YOUR OWN STYLE TO FINLEY AND FRIENDS!

For more coloring pages, visit:

thelegendofpineapplecove.com/book1

ABOUT THE AUTHOR

MARINA J. BOWMAN is a writer and explorer who travels the world searching for wildly fantastical stories to share with her readers. Ever since she was a child, she has been fascinated with uncovering long lost secrets and chasing the mythical, magical, and supernatural. For her current story, Marina is investigating Pineapple Cove, a mysterious island located somewhere in the Atlantic.

Marina enjoys sailing, flying, and nearly all other forms of transportation. She never strays far from the ocean for long, as it brings her both inspiration and peace. She stays away from the spotlight to maintain privacy and ensure the more unpleasant secrets she uncovers don't catch up with her.

As a matter of survival, Marina nearly always communicates with the public through her representative, Devin Cowick. Ms. Cowick is an entrepreneur who shares Marina's passion for travel and creative storytelling and is the co-founder of Code Pineapple.

Marina's last name is pronounced baʊmən, and rhymes with "now then."